The Colony of Delaware
A Primary Source History

Jake Miller

The Rosen Publishing Group's
PowerKids Press™
New York

Published in 2006 by The Rosen Publishing Group, Inc.
29 East 21st Street, New York, NY 10010

First Edition

Editor: Jennifer Way
Book Design: Ginny Chu
Photo Researcher: Gabriel Caplan

Photo Credits: Cover and title page "Landing of the DeVries Colony at Swaanendael, Lewes, Delaware" by Stanley Arthurs, Permanent Collection of the University of Delaware; p. 4 Library of Congress Geography and Map Division; p. 4 (inset) Courtesy of The Library of Virginia; p. 6 Photography: National Archives, Sweden, Kurt Eriksson; p. 6 (inset) The Art Archive / Gripsholm Castle Sweden / Dagli Orti (A); p. 7 Courtesy of the Friends of the Swedish Cabin; p. 8 Art Resource, NY; pp. 8 (inset), 18 Delaware Public Archives; p. 10 Photo courtesy of Enoch Pratt Free Library/State Library Resource Center, Baltimore, Maryland; p. 10 (inset) The New York Public Library / Art Resource, NY; p. 12 The Granger Collection, New York; p. 12 (inset) Money Museum, Federal Reserve Bank of Richmond; p. 14 (left) Library of Congress Prints and Photographs Division; p. 14 (right) Reproduced with permission from Readex, a division of NewsBank, inc., and the American Antiquarian Society; p. 16 Photo by Will Brown, courtesy of Christ Church in Philadelphia; pp. 16 (inset), 18 (inset) Independence National Historical Park; p. 20 © Chicago Historical Society, Chicago, USA/Bridgeman Art Library; p.20 (inset) Historical Society of Delaware.

Library of Congress Cataloging-in-Publication Data

Miller, Jake.
  The colony of Delaware : a primary source history / Jake Miller.
    p. cm. — (Primary source library of the thirteen colonies and the Lost Colony)
  Includes index.
  ISBN 1-4042-3033-5 (library binding)
  1. Delaware—History—Colonial period, ca. 1600–1775—Juvenile literature. 2. Delaware—History—1775–1865—Juvenile literature.
I. Title.

  F167.M55 2006
  975.1'02—dc22
                                                    2004029327

Manufactured in the United States of America

Contents

This map of the Delaware Bay from around 1639 was created by the Dutch East India Company. The Netherlands had claimed the land near the bay in 1609. Inset: Thomas West, Lord De La Warr, lived from 1577 to 1618.

Europe Finds Delaware

The colony of Delaware was located in the middle of the Atlantic coast of North America. Henry Hudson, an English captain working for the Dutch, claimed the area from today's Delaware to New York for the Netherlands in 1609. Native Americans already lived on the land the Europeans were claiming. The largest group of Native Americans in Delaware was a Native American group called the Lenni-Lenape.

The first recorded European to sail into Delaware Bay was the Englishman Samuel Argall. In 1610, Argall's ship had been blown off course by a storm, and he found himself in an uncharted bay. He named both the bay and the river that flowed into it Delaware, in honor of Lord De La Warr, the governor of Virginia.

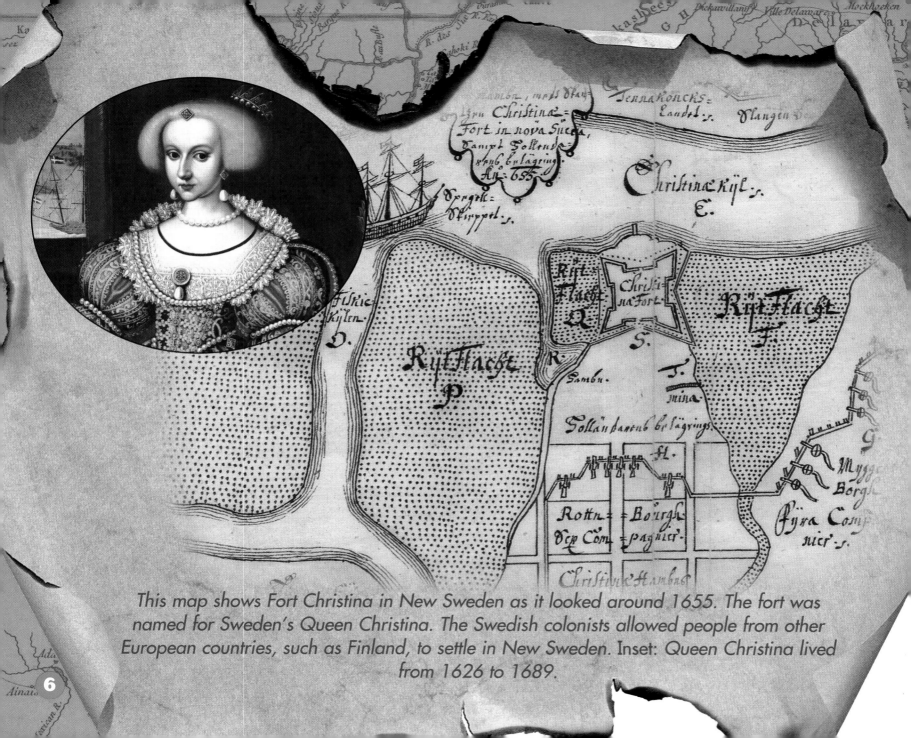

This map shows Fort Christina in New Sweden as it looked around 1655. The fort was named for Sweden's Queen Christina. The Swedish colonists allowed people from other European countries, such as Finland, to settle in New Sweden. Inset: Queen Christina lived from 1626 to 1689.

New Sweden and New Netherlands

After Argall other Europeans came to the Delaware Bay to trade but did not settle. A group of Dutch settlers came in 1631, but the colony failed after a year.

In 1638, a group of Swedes began a colony called New Sweden in today's Wilmington, Delaware. The Dutch had a colony nearby called New Netherlands. The Dutch did not like the Swedes settling on the land that they had claimed. In 1655, Peter Stuyvesant sailed from New Netherlands and took control of New Sweden. The Swedish and Finnish colonists stayed, but the land was now controlled by the Netherlands.

New Sweden's Finnish settlers made an important addition to American society. They brought the idea of building log cabins with them from the forests of Finland. For the next 200 years, settlers in America often made a log cabin, like the one shown above, for their first home.

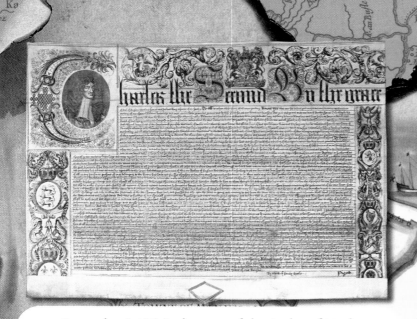

"This indenture made the four and Twentieth day of August . . .1682 betweene . . . James Duke of York and . . .William Penn. . . . Witnesseth That his said Royall Highness out of a speciall regarde to the memory and many faithfull and eminent Services heretofore performed by the said Sr William Penn. . . . lett unto said William Penn all that tract of Land upon Delaware River and Bay . . . "

The passage above says that on August 20, 1682, the Duke of York gave land on the Delaware River and the Delaware Bay to William Penn. This was to honor the Penn family for their father's service to the Crown.

This 1664 map shows Manhattan, which like Delaware had been part of New Netherlands. In 1664, New Netherlands was taken over by England and renamed New York. Inset: The 1682 Indenture of the Duke of York granted land to the Penn family. This land would later become Delaware. An indenture is a formal contract.

An English Colony on the Delaware Bay

Delaware did not remain a part of New Netherlands for long. In 1664, the British took over New Netherlands, which included Delaware. New Netherlands was renamed New York in honor of James Stuart, the Duke of York, the brother of England's king.

In 1682, the Duke of York gave the land around the Delaware Bay to William Penn because he owed money to the Penn family. The land then became part of Penn's **proprietary colony** of Pennsylvania. Penn was a **Quaker** who wanted to start a colony where members of his religion could live by their beliefs. The three counties that now make up Delaware were known as the Low Counties of Pennsylvania.

The inset map contains the following text:

Gent Mag Nov. 1769.

PENNSILVANIA

Philadelphia

40

NEW JERSEY

Greenwich

Castle

Baltimore

DELAWARE BAY

Chester R.

Dover

Cape May

39

CHESOPEAK BAY

Annapolis

Lewes

Indian R.

38

Potowmack R.

Pt Anne

VIRGINIA

THE ATLANTIC OCEAN

Rappahanock R.

York R.

James R.

Cape Charles

The Capes of Virginia

37

Miles.

A MAP
of that Part of
AMERICA
where a Degree of
LATITUDE
was Measured for the
Royal Society:
By Cha. Mason & Jere. Dixon.

Charles Calvert, the third Lord Baltimore, claimed that William Penn's Delaware lands belonged to his Maryland colony. This disagreement lasted more than 70 years. Inset: Charles Mason and Jeremiah Dixon's 1769 map defined the borders between Maryland, Delaware, and Pennsylvania, ending the Baltimore-Penn disagreement.

Delaware Separates from Pennsylvania

In the 1680s, there were disagreements about who controlled Delaware. Lord Baltimore, the governor of Maryland, believed Delaware was included under Maryland's **charter**. This was because the maps from that time were not always correct. Charters that had been drawn from these maps sometimes added to the uncertainty.

In 1704, Delaware formed its own government to pass laws and taxes. The Penn family still owned the colony, however, and appointed a governor to rule both Pennsylvania and Delaware.

The disagreement between Maryland and Pennsylvania was settled in 1769, when mapmakers Charles Mason and Jeremiah Dixon made a map that clearly defined the borders between Maryland, Delaware, and Pennsylvania.

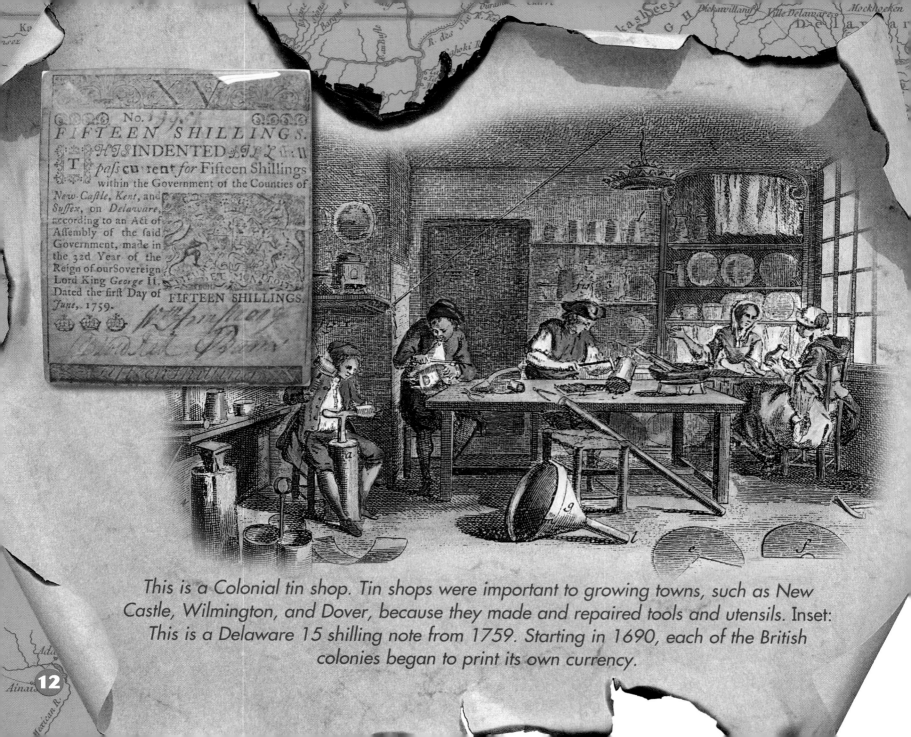

This is a Colonial tin shop. Tin shops were important to growing towns, such as New Castle, Wilmington, and Dover, because they made and repaired tools and utensils. Inset: This is a Delaware 15 shilling note from 1759. Starting in 1690, each of the British colonies began to print its own currency.

Delaware Succeeds

In the North American colonies that were settled in the early 1600s, such as those in Massachusetts and Virginia, many colonists died in the early years. Many died from illness or died of hunger because they could not grow enough food. Often other colonies were not nearby to trade with for supplies. Colonies that were settled a bit later, such as Delaware, could trade with the nearby colonies to make money to buy supplies.

By the 1700s, Delaware was successful. Many settlers were farmers who grew crops such as corn or wheat. Other settlers built mills to turn these grains into flour. Leather-making and shipbuilding businesses grew in Wilmington. The people of Delaware also sold their goods to other colonies, to Britain, and to other countries.

THE LAMENTATION, OF PENNSYLVANIA,

On Account of the *Stamp-Act*, together with the Prayer of *J---n H------ws.*

O! Lord have Mercy on thy own Elect in this and other Provinces,
For Rain now appears in every one their Eyes, and set them all vast mad.

ARISE my Boys, awake and hear my Song,
Your Spirits cheer, your Liberty not gone,
Though *England* strives to put his Stamp on you,
We'll drive the *Scotch* Mist back, from whence it blew,
This *Highland* Plot 'twas first that made the Scheme;
A spiteful Dog, who's Teeth is very keen,
To strive to ruin *England*, Still but he,
Shall dance without a Head you all shall see.
Our *English* Natives never did invent,
To hurt their Fellow Subjects, but prevent.
No *GEORGE* our *British* KING, did never strive;
To hurt his Kingdom, but to make it drive.
And now before we will receive the Stamp,
We'll make the *Scotch* Dogs all to have the Cramp.
No Traitor never shall our Courage fade,
Nor STAMPS for PHILADELPHIA then be made.
For Liberty and Property we'll have,
And stand to it with Courage, then so brave.
If *J.---y H------ws*, don't the *Stamp* refuse,
I wish he may be thus abus'd.
Grant Heaven, that he may never go without,
The Rheumatism, Itch, the Pox or Gout.
May he be hamper'd with some ugly Witch,
And die at last in some curst foulsome Ditch.
Without the Benefit of Psalms or Hymnes,
And Crouds of Crows devour his rotten Limbs.
May wanton Boys, to Town his Bones convey,
To make a Bonfire on a Rejoicing Day.

The paper has been given gratis to some parties in this region that
sought a square piece of any paper from the man who has his
paying a ... ...

From The Lamentation of Pennsylvania

"Arise my Boys, awake and hear my Song,
Your Spirits cheer, your Liberty not gone,
Though England strives to put his Stamp on you,
We'll drive the Scotch Mist back from whence it blew."

The first four lines of the Lamentation tell the reader the purpose of the poem. The writer asks that people listen to the poem and work together to bring an end to the Stamp Act. Lamentation means to mourn for something.

John Dickinson served in both Delaware's and Pennsylvania's Colonial governments. He wrote articles against the new British laws. Inset: "The Lamentation of Pennsylvania" makes fun of the Stamp Act, which was passed in 1765. This unpopular tax on paper goods was ended the following year. The "Pennsylvania" in the poem's title includes Pennsylvania and Delaware.

Delaware Objects to Unfair Taxes

After the **French and Indian War**, which was fought in North America, the British wanted the colonies to help pay for its costs. To raise money they passed taxes, such as the Stamp Act. The colonists did not think it was fair for **Parliament** to pass taxes, because the colonies were not **represented** in Parliament.

The colonies objected to the new taxes. Delaware's government refused to collect them, and people **boycotted** British goods. In the 1770s, each colony set up a **Committee of Correspondence** so that it could talk about ways to work out its problems with Britain. Caesar Rodney and George Read were on Delaware's committee. The committees did not solve the colonies' problems with Britain, but they were an important step toward bringing the colonies together to fight the British.

The First Continental Congress met at Carpenter's Hall in Philadelphia, Pennsylvania, on September 5, 1774. One of the things Delaware did after Congress met was to form Committees of Inspection. Inset: Thomas McKean was one of the men from Delaware at Congress.

ATLAN

Delaware at the Continental Congress

In 1774, the Committees of Correspondence called a Continental Congress in Philadelphia, Pennsylvania. The leaders of the colonies wanted to meet to talk about their worsening relationships with Great Britain. Delaware sent George Read, Caesar Rodney, and Thomas McKean. One thing the colonies agreed to do was to continue boycotting British goods. Delaware even formed Committees of Inspection to make sure that people in the colony honored the boycott. The colonies hoped that boycotts would convince the British to treat the colonies fairly.

In 1775, the colonies' relationship with Britain got even worse. The British had sent troops to Massachusetts to stop the colonists' protests, and the two sides had begun to fight. This was the beginning of the **American Revolution**.

This plaque in Wilmington, Delaware, honors Caesar Rodney's arrival to vote for the Declaration of Independence. Inset: George Read thought it would be better for the colonies to work out their differences with Britain instead of fighting a war. He did not think colonists would support the war because many people depended on trade with Britain for their living.

Independence for Delaware

On June 15, 1776, the Continental Congress met again in Philadelphia to decide whether to write the **Declaration of Independence**. George Read opposed the declaration. Caesar Rodney and Thomas McKean supported the declaration. On the day of the vote only McKean and Read were in Philadelphia. Delaware's vote would be tied, one in favor and one against.

When a messenger reached Rodney and told him that the vote had been called, he rushed back to Philadelphia from Delaware on horseback. As it turned out, Read changed his mind and all three signed the Declaration of Independence. When Delaware's government voted to declare its independence from Britain, it also voted to break away from Pennsylvania. Delaware was finally an independent state.

The Battle of Cowpens, shown in this painting, was fought in South Carolina in 1781. The Delaware Regiment was one of the groups of Continental army troops that helped bring about this Colonial win. Inset: Thomas Robinson was one of Delaware's biggest supporters of the loyalist cause.

Delaware in the American Revolution

During the American Revolution, many people in Delaware were loyalists. They did not observe boycotts and they sold supplies to the British. This caused fighting between loyalists and patriots, who backed the Revolution.

The only Revolutionary battle fought in Delaware was a patriot loss at Cooch's Bridge, on September 3, 1777. Men from Delaware fought with the Continental army throughout the war, though. The Delaware Regiment fought in the South, including the Battle of Camden in South Carolina in August 1780, and the Battle of Cowpens in South Carolina in January 1781. Delaware troops were also at the Battle of Yorktown, Virginia, where the patriot win ended the fighting on October 17, 1781. The war officially ended in 1783, when the Treaty of Paris was signed.

The First State

The **Articles of Confederation** had governed the colonies during the Revolution, but they were not useful for running the new nation. For example, there were no laws to govern trade between states or to collect taxes. The United States needed a government that would allow the states to work as a nation.

Delaware was one of five states to send representatives to the Annapolis Convention in Maryland in September 1786. The convention was called to go over the rules to govern trade. The representatives soon realized that they would need to write a new **constitution**. They called the states together for a **Constitutional Convention** in May 1787. On December 7, 1787, Delaware was the first of the states to approve the new Constitution and join the United States. .

Glossary

American Revolution (uh-MER-uh-ken reh-vuh-LOO-shun) Battles that soldiers from the colonies fought against Britain for freedom, from 1775 to 1783.

Articles of Confederation (AR-tih-kulz UV kun-feh-deh-RAY-shun) The laws that governed the United States before the Constitution was created.

boycotted (BOY-kot-ed) To have refused to buy from or deal with a person, nation, or business.

charter (CHAR-tur) An official agreement giving someone permission to do something.

Committee of Correspondence (kuh-MIH-tee UV kor-eh-SPAHN-dens) A group of leaders in the colonies who came together to talk about freedom from England. The committees became the early governing bodies for the colonies as they became states.

constitution (kon-stih-TOO-shun) The basic rules by which a country or a state is governed.

Constitutional Convention (kon-stih-TOO-shuh-nul kun-VEN-shun) The political body that met in the summer of 1787 to create the U.S. Constitution.

Declaration of Independence (deh-kluh-RAY-shun UV in-duh-PEN-dints) An official announcement signed on July 4, 1776, in which American colonists stated they were free of British rule.

French and Indian War (FRENCH AND IN-dee-in WOR) The battles fought between 1754 and 1763 by England, France, and Native Americans for control of North America.

Parliament (PAR-lih-mint) The group in England that makes the country's laws.

proprietary colony (pruh-PRY-uh-tehr-ee KAH-luh-nee) A privately owned colony or settlement.

Quaker (KWAY-kur) A person who belongs to a faith that believes in equality for all people, strong families and communities, and peace.

represented (reh-prih-ZENT-ed) Had people to speak for a group in Parliament or Congress.

23

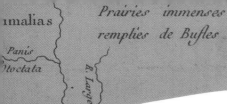

Index

Primary Sources

Page 4. *Caert vande Svydt Rivier in Niew Nederland.* Pen-and-ink watercolor map, circa 1639, Joan Vinckeboons, Library of Congress Geography and Map Division, Washington, D.C. **Page 6.** *Stadhen Christina Fort in Nova Svecia.* Pen-and-ink map, 1691, Peter Lindestrom, National Archives (Riksarkivet), Sweden. **Page 6. Inset.** *Queen Christina* (detail). Oil-on-canvas painting, 17th century, Jacob Heinlich, The National Museum of Fine Arts, Stockholm, Sweden. **Page 8. Inset.** *Indenture of the Duke of York* (detail). 1682, Delaware Public Archives, Dover, Delaware. **Page 10.** *Charles Calvert, Third Lord Baltimore.* Painting, circa 1647–1715, Sir Godfrey Kneller, Enoch Pratt Free Library, Baltimore, Maryland. **Page 10. Inset.** Map. Hand-colored, 1769, Charles Mason, New York Public Library. **Page 12. Inset.** Delaware fifteen-shilling note. June 1, 1759, Federal Museum, Richmond, Virginia. **Page 14.** *The patriotic American Farmer J-n D-k-ns-n Esqr. Barrister at law.* Print, circa 1870 after 1772 illustration, R. Bell, Library of Congress, Washington, D.C. **Page 14. Inset.** *Lamentation of Pennsylvania.* Broadside, 1765, Anthony Armbuster. **Page 16. Inset.** *Thomas McKean* (detail). Painting, 1797, Charles Willson Peale. **Page 20.** *Colonel William Washington at the Battle of Cowpens, January 17, 1781.* Oil-on-canvas painting, circa late 18th century, Anonymous, Chicago Historical Society.

Web Sites

Due to the changing nature of Internet links, PowerKids Press has developed an online list of Web sites related to the subject of this book. This site is updated regularly. Please use this link to access the list: www.powerkidslinks.com/pstclc/delaware/